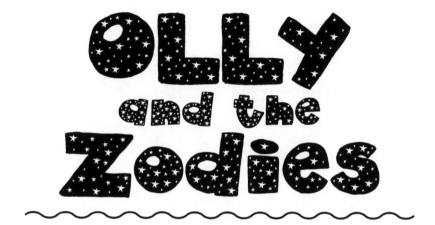

OLLY and the Zodies

Written by
EMMANUEL KING

ARCHWAY
PUBLISHING

Archway Publishing books may be ordered through booksellers or by contacting:

Archway Publishing
1663 Liberty Drive
Bloomington, IN 47403
www.archwaypublishing.com
1 (888) 242-5904

ISBN: 978-1-4808-1898-9 (sc)
ISBN: 978-1-4808-1897-2 (e)

Library of Congress Control Number: 2015908344

Print information available on the last page.

Archway Publishing rev. date: 7/1/2015

CONTENTS

CHAPTER ONE

Land of the Zodies

There was once a little girl named Ellen Campbell. She was a kind-hearted and warm little girl who loved new and exciting things. Not long ago, Ellen was celebrating her eighth birthday at her house where she lived with her mother and father. At her party were aunts and uncles and friends from school. Ellen's birthday is during the summer, so she was happy to see her classmates again.

Ellen was enjoying her birthday party. She especially enjoyed the presents and the ice cream cake. Ice cream cake is her favorite. It's mine as well but enough about me. Even though she was very happy on her special day, Ellen couldn't help but be a bit suspicious. For one thing,

Ellen's mother was keeping people, especially Ellen, from going into the backyard. Another thing Ellen or anyone else couldn't help but notice were the bandages that covered her father's hands.

Ellen is a very smart girl, you must understand. She knew what was going on. Her parents had a big surprise gift out in the backyard that they were saving for last. Her father, who she knew very well, liked to build things. He had built a birdhouse once that was home to a mother and her baby birds. He had never hurt himself before so Ellen thought her gift must be big if her father needed bandages after working on it, whatever it was.

Ellen was quite eager to find out what the big surprise was. She felt that if she did not find out right away, she would most certainly burst into a cadrillion tiny pieces. If that happened, she knew she would never know what the surprise was and she knew there was a surprise. She was a very smart girl.

She wanted the surprise so greatly that she opened all gifts quickly. She played games with the others she knew wouldn't take very long. She also ate her ice cream cake at a speed that only resulted in an ice cream headache. Aren't those awful?

"Why does something so wonderful have to cause something so terrible" wondered Ellen to herself.

"Everyone, there is one last gift for Ellen to open! Everybody follow me out back!" shouted her mother.

"Finally" Ellen whispered.

There was a short delay in getting to the backyard. Ellen's father was having trouble turning the door knob because his hands were covered in bandages. It was a funny, yet sad, yet funny sight to see. Thankfully, Ellen's mother opened the door and all the guests walked outside. Towards the back of the yard, was something underneath a large sheet. This was it. Soon Ellen would have her special gift. She was so excited.

"Ellen," called her mother. "This is your birthday gift from your father and I."

At this point, you should know, the plan was to have Ellen's father remove the sheet and reveal her gift. As you already know, he's having difficulty with his hands. The difficulty being that they are of no use to him. This was not a worry for Ellen. She grabbed hold of the sheet and pulled like no one had ever pulled before or since.

The sheet had been pulled away and was in a clump on the ground. Ellen stared with her jaw agape. Before her was a green playhouse big enough to do a cartwheel in. She couldn't believe it. Ellen was so happy. She had her very own playhouse. Earlier in the year, when Ellen and her parents were watching television together, she saw a girl playing in a playhouse and said she wished she had one. Now she did. Ellen turned to her mother.

"Your father built it and I painted it," her mother said.

"Thank you, mommy!" Ellen said, as she hugged her mother. Then she ran to her father and hugged him.

"Thank you, daddy! Can I go in?!," she asked excitedly.

"Of course you can, sweetie."

Ellen's hand was pushing the door open before her father finished saying "course." Once she was inside, Ellen looked and walked around. There were bean bags to sit on and two closed windows, one on the left and one on the right side of the house. On the walls and roof were paintings of the zodiac signs. Ellen and her mother liked to look up into the sky at night with a telescope and see the constellations or collection of stars that look like different animals or objects. Some people believe that each person has a sign connected to their birth. Her mother told her she was a Leo. Ellen liked hearing that because a Leo was a lion and lions were kings of the jungle.

Ellen looked all around the playhouse for the sign of the Leo. Suddenly, she heard scratching at the door. Then it stopped. No dog had been invited to the party so she couldn't figure out what was doing the scratching. When Ellen slowly opened the door, she was treated to another surprise. She was no longer in her backyard.

"Where am I? Mommy? Daddy?" she called as she stepped outside. Ellen had no idea where she was. She had no idea how she got there. Those are scary situations to not have an idea about. Even scarier was her next thought.

"How do I get back home?" she wondered.

Ellen looked all around her. She and her playhouse stood in the middle of a beautiful green field with a forest to the right. Ellen couldn't believe what she saw in the distance. One part of the land in the distance looked as though it were stuck in winter time. Snow was falling and covered the ground and trees. Right next to that was a patch of land where it seemed to be autumn all the time. The leaves on the trees were the colors of the rainbow. Next to that, there was a beach with palm trees all around.

Ellen was very frightened that she was no longer safe in her backyard with her parents celebrating her birthday. However, there was another feeling right alongside her fear. It was a feeling that something exciting might soon happen in this world that was not her own. Ellen loved new things. Oftentimes, new things meant fun experiences. At the time, Ellen was feeling forty-nine percent excited and fifty-one percent frightened.

As much as Ellen wanted to know about this strange world she found herself in, she thought the best thing to do was to go back inside her playhouse.

"The playhouse brought me here. Maybe it can take me home," she said.

That seems a very smart thought to me. I would do the same thing if I could fit inside a playhouse to begin with. When Ellen turned around to head for her playhouse, she instantly felt ninety-nine percent frightened and one percent excited because standing before her was a lion, an odd looking lion. Ellen thought so too as she stared at him and he stared at her thinking she was odd. Why was he odd looking, you ask? Well, for one thing, his body was red. For another thing, he was standing on two feet like you and I do. I'm assuming only two footed individuals are reading this book. For still another thing, his mane, which was a golden yellow or a yellowish gold, looked like fluffy cotton candy. The odd lion became more odd because he began to speak.

"Hello, my name is Olly. Nice to meet you. If you're a bad person, I'll have to eat you," said the lion whose name is Olly, smiling.

Ellen had a number of things to get used to before she could speak. She was in a strange world with no one she knew. In front of her was a lion; a red lion; a red talking lion. Finally she spoke.

"I'm not a bad person," she said.

"Good, because I'm full. Who are you?" asked Olly.

"I'm Ellen Campbell."

"My full name is Ollilio N. Lion. Everyone calls me Olly because I tell them to."

"Everyone does what you tell them?" asked Ellen.

"I'm the Leo. People have to listen to me. I'm in charge."

"My mom says I'm a Leo, too," Ellen stated proudly.

"You don't look like a Leo," said Olly as he studied Ellen.

"You don't look like any lion I've seen. How come you're red?"

"Because I want to be!"

"You chose to be red?" asked Ellen surprised.

"I didn't want to follow and be like other lions," Olly said with pride.

Almost everything Olly said was said with pride. And he took pride in that. Even though Ellen was enjoying the fact that she was having a conversation with a lion, she had an important question.

"Where am I?" she asked.

"The land of the Zodies!" answered Olly. "This is where the members of the zodiac live.

"The land of the Zodies," repeated Ellen.

"That's right! I am the Leo of the zodiac!" exclaimed Olly. "You don't look like a Leo, but a Leo wouldn't lie and say he was if he wasn't. You must be a Leo from the human world."

"Yes! I was there a little while ago at my birthday party. I turned eight today. How old are you?

"I'm as old as I am," responded Olly.

Even though she just met Olly, Ellen felt that that would be the best answer to the question she would get. She decided to be brave and ask another question.

"Do you know how to get me back to my world?"

"Of course I do, I think," said the almost sure lion. "If you help me, I will make sure you get back to your world."

"You promise?!"

That did it. Ellen had offended Olly.

"Every statement a Leo makes is a promise!" Olly informed her.

"Okay, I'll help you."

"Good. Now off we go!" exclaimed Olly as he turned and made his way toward the forest with Ellen at his side. "As the mighty Leo, it is my duty to inform you, that we are now friends."

Ellen had never been told she was friends with anyone before. She thought Olly seemed like a nice enough talking lion.

"Oh! Okay, we're friends,"she accepted as the two entered the forest.

"Sorry I scratched your door," apologized Olly.

"So that was you. That's okay."

"I was looking for my roar. Did you hear it in your world?" asked Olly.

"No...Your roar?"

"Yes. I lost it yesterday and I haven't been able to find it."

"How did you lose your roar?"

"Haven't you heard of someone losing their voice?"

"Yes," answered Ellen.

"Well, when I lost my roar, it ran way."

"Well, I'll help you find it," said Ellen.

"I almost caught it earlier. A frog had it and was scaring bugs to death with it. The frog would roar and the flies would drop like flies. I have to find my roar. Without it, I can't truly call myself a lion."

"Your roar is just a sound you make. Even if you can't roar, you're still a Leo, a cute little red Leo."

Olly did not like being called cute.

"The audacity of you to call me cute. I'll have you know that I am ferocious!" exclaimed Olly, trying his best to sound scary.

"You are! You are! I'm sorry I called you cute."

"It's okay. I forgive you," accepted Olly, looking very cute. "You say you are a Leo. Let me hear you roar."

Ellen did her very best to squeak out a roar. "Rrroaarrr!"

That did it. Ellen offended Olly a third time and they had only just met. First, she questioned his word. Then she called him cute. Now this: she has roared disappointingly.

"That is the saddest thing I have ever heard."

"I am a Leo but I'm also human," Ellen offered as an excuse.

"What sounds do humans make?"

"I don't know. Human sounds, I guess."

"That's no good. After we find my roar, we'll find a sound for you to make."

After walking for a short time in the forest, the two new friends stopped at a stream.

"This is the Pisces Stream. It is home to sisters Penelope and Isis Pisces," explained Olly.

"Do you think they will know where your roar is?" Ellen asked.

"I doubt it. These two are rarely of any help but I'm desperate to get my roar back. I'd be happy if when I opened my mouth, silence didn't come out. Oh! Be careful not to let the water from the stream touch you. Not even one drop," warned Olly.

"Why?"

"If you touch the water from the Pisces Stream, you take on the mood of the Pisces sisters and they are rarely in a happy mood. So watch out."

Ellen was nervous yet excited to meet new creatures in this strange land. Olly stood on the bank of thee stream and outstretched his arms.

"I, Olly the Leo, summon the Pisces sisters!"

Suddenly, the water began to bubble and glow with a bright light. Then two large bubbles emerged and in each was a large fish that appeared to Ellen to be wearing make-up and lipstick and had their hair done in a fancy, crazy style.

"Look, Isis, sister," said Penelope.

"By golly, it's Olly, Penelope, sister," said Isis.

"He has a friend with him, Isis."

"You're right, Penelope."

"I do not believe she is a Zodie, Isis."

"I'm sure you're right, Penelope."

"My name is Ellen. I'm from the human world. It's nice to meet the two of you."

"The non Zodie girl speaks, Isis, sister."

"She does indeed, Penelope, sister."

"She can speak but don't ask her to roar because when she does, it's a puny kind of roar and will make you sad to hear it," said Olly.

"We don't want to be sad, do we, Isis?"

"Not at all, Penelope."

"We're here because I need your help," said Olly. "I have lost my roar and I was wondering if you might know where it is."

"Olly really wants his roar and it would be nice if you could help us," added Ellen.

"We do not know where your roar is, but we would love to help you," said Penelope.

"Nothing would make us happier than to help you," said Isis.

"We'd be immensely happy to help you look, wouldn't we, Isis, sister?"

"We'd be immeasurably happy, Penelope, sister."

"Thank you," said Ellen.

"Isis, sister, I'll swim up this end of the stream and listen for Olly's roar."

"Excellent idea, Penelope, sister. You do that and I'll swim down that end and listen for Olly's roar."

Ellen was very happy she had met two very nice fish ladies who were going to help. When she looked beside her to Olly, she saw he didn't look very grateful for Penelope and Isis's kindness. She would soon learn why. Just as the two fish were about to take off in opposite directions in their bubbles, it appeared the same thought popped into their fish heads.

"Wait a moment!" both sisters said together.

"Isis, sister?"

"Yes, Penelope, sister?"

"We aren't in need of a roar, are we?"

"I don't believe so. I don't need a roar, Penelope, sister. Do you?"

"I do not, Isis, sister."

"If neither of us needs a roar, then why in water should we go looking for one, Penelope, sister?"

"Excellent question, Isis."

"Then we shouldn't, Penelope."

"Then we won't, Isis."

Ellen was stunned. Olly was not.

"Just because you don't need a roar or just because it's not your roar doesn't mean you can't help! You're supposed to help because it's good to help not because of what's in it for you! It's wrong of you not to help. I'm sorry but you two are bad fish!" shouted Ellen.

"How could you say that?" the sisters said together.

"We happen to be very kind fish. Right, Isis?"

"When it suits us, yes, Penelope."

"I am hurt to my gills that you could say such a thing," said Penelope.

"I feel the hurt in my fins," said Isis.

Ellen began to feel a little sad that she had hurt the Pisces sisters' feelings.

"Isis, sister, I'm going to be sad up that end of the stream."

"While you do that, Penelope, sister, I'll be sad down this end of the stream."

The bubble that each sister was in, returned to the water and once it was submerged, they swam to opposite ends and began to be sad.

"Don't worry, Ellen," said Olly. "Those two weren't going to be much help to us no matter what you said. The Pisces sisters only help if it's something they're interested in. Normally I wouldn't have bothered, but like I said earlier, I'm desperate."

The two left the Pisces Stream and began listening for Olly's roar all over the forest. After all this listening on the ground, Olly decided they should try listening from a higher place. Olly picked out a tree and was up to the top in a dash which is very fast. Ellen tried her best but couldn't get very far up the tree without sliding back to the ground.

"I can't climb as well as you can!" Ellen shouted up to Olly.

"Don't be silly! If you're having trouble, just ask the tree for help!" he shouted back down.

This is a very strange world indeed Ellen thought. If a lion can be red and fish can talk, why shouldn't a tree assist her ascent. Ellen thought she'd give it a try.

"Excuse me, mister or miss tree. Would you mind helping me?" asked Ellen politely.

All of a sudden, one large branch swung down in front

of Ellen. She sat down on it and the branch lifted her up and placed her next to Olly on another of its branches.

"Don't trees do that where you're from?" Olly asked.

"No they do not," answered Ellen.

"You must live in a strange world" concluded Olly. "If anybody knows the goings on in a forest, it's the birds. Let's see what they know."

Behind Olly were several birds in a row on the same branch.

"Hello, birds! It's me, Olly! Unfortunately, I am without my roar today. But, I am with a new friend. This is Ellen."

"Hello, birds," greeted Ellen.

"As I said, I have no roar. It ran away, the silly thing. I was wondering if any of you might know where my roar might be."

"Tweetings, Olly. Tweetings, Ellen. At the moment, we're dealing with a crises that might have to do with your missing roar," said an important looking bird. "It seems earlier today, one of our brethren was about to make lunch of a seemingly unsuspecting worm, when suddenly, the worm let out such a powerful roar, that it terrified the poor soul into quite an agitated state. It gave him the scare of his little birdy life."

"Will he be okay?" asked Ellen.

"We believe in time he will recover, yes," replied the bird.

"Can we see him?" asked Olly.

"Yes, but please do not say the word, roar. It upsets him."

The important bird pointed to a hole in the tree behind Ellen, indicating where the traumatized bird was. Olly climbed over Ellen and gently stuck his head in the hole.

"Hello, how are you?" Olly asked the poor bird.

"I'm fine, I suppose," he said weakly.

"Can you tell me where the incident happened with the worm?"

"It was in the clearing, just a little walk from here. That's where it happened."

"That's where the worm roared?" asked Olly.

That's when the bird snapped.

"Roar! Roar!! Roaring worm!!!" repeated the bird as it flew around the hole, out the hole and then fainted. The poor bird dropped like a rock out of the sky, landing with a 'FLUMPH!'

Ellen and Olly looked worried.

"It's okay," said the important bird. "He landed in a pile of leaves we placed at the bottom of the tree. That's the third time he's done that after hearing the word roar."

"Sorry about that," said Olly. "Let's go, Ellen!"

"Thank you, birds!" said Ellen as she and Olly climbed down the tree.

"Yeah, thanks! We're off to find my roar!" Olly added as the two departed.

"Roaring worm!" shouted the bird from the pile of leaves.

Ellen and Olly arrived at the clearing where the bird was scared by the worm. The two friends walked around the clearing listening for any sign of Olly's lost roar. Suddenly, there was a mighty roar and from a tiny hole in the ground, crawled at least twelve worms. Whatever the worm equivalent to running is, that's what they were doing. They all looked terrified.

"Slither for your lives!" screamed one worm.

"Oh, the wormanity!" screamed another.

Olly and Ellen ran to the hole all the worms were fleeing.

"Is there a worm with a roar down there?" Olly asked one.

"There sure is and he's gone crazy with power!" said the worm as it slithered off.

"Hey, you roaring worm! Come out here right now!" Olly shouted down the hole.

A moment later, the last worm slithered out with a loud roar and was greeted by a sympathetic looking Ellen and a stern looking Olly.

"I know you have my roar, worm, so you better give it back!" demanded Olly.

"No way! This roar is the best thing that's ever happened to me," said the worm.

"What do you mean?" asked Ellen.

"Did you see how all the other worms ran off when I roared? That's the power of my roar. I can get them to do whatever I want now."

"The roar doesn't belong to you!" exclaimed Olly.

"It does now" said the worm.

"I don't understand," said Ellen. "Why would you want your worm friends to do things for you or with you only because they're scared of you? People and worms will be happy to do nice things for you if you're nice to them first. Besides that, you just scared all the other worms away. There's no one around to listen to you with or without a roar. If you can get them to listen again, it should be to the worm you, not the roar."

The worm thought about it and realized Ellen was right. He didn't want fear to be the reason he got respect.

"Okay, you're right," said the worm. "I'm really sorry, Mr. Lion."

"My name is Olly and I accept your apology."

"You're a very good little worm" added Ellen.

"Thank you," accepted the worm.

"How will you get your roar out of him?" asked Ellen.

"Easy. He has to cough it up," answered Olly.

"Cough it up?" Ellen repeated.

"Like he's choking on a piece of pie," said Olly as he got close to the tiny worm. "Pretend my roar is at the back of your throat and then just cough it up."

The worm imagined the roar at the back of its throat. Please don't ask me, reader, where on a worm its throat is. I could not tell you. Thankfully, this worm knew. Then the worm began to cough and a glowing orb emerged from his mouth. Ellen realized this must be the form Olly's roar takes. The orb floated in midair for a moment before Olly gobbled it up like, well, like a hungry lion. Olly then let out a mighty roar.

"Rrrroooaaarrr!!"

Ellen was amazed that such a sound could come out of a little lion.

"Now people will know it's me when they see me," said Olly.

Ellen and Olly made their way out of the forest and were standing outside her playhouse once again.

"I'm glad you found your roar, Olly."

"Thank you for helping, Ellen. You make a good Leo even though your roar makes my heart cry."

"I'll work on it and I promise it'll get better," Ellen vowed.

"Good, because if you don't improve, I will not allow you to be a Leo anymore."

"Okay. I've had fun, but I really want to go home. My parents are probably worried about me."

"They won't even know you've gone."

"What do you mean?" asked a confused Ellen.

"When you return to your human world, you'll only have been in your playhouse for a minute or two. Time doesn't flow at the same speed here."

"Really?"

"Of course, really! Leo's never lie! Or do liars never Leo? No, that's silly. Leo's never lie!"

"Right. Now how do I get home?"

"That is very simple," Olly said. "All you have to do is go in your playhouse, close the door and wish to be back home."

"That's all?" Ellen asked.

"That is all. Before you were transported here, what were you doing?"

"I was in my playhouse looking at the zodiac signs on the roof and walls. I looked and looked but I couldn't find the Leo."

"You were looking for me, so your playhouse brought you to me. Now you want to go home, so go in, think of home, and home you will be."

"Okay, thank you, Olly!"

"Just one moment, Ellen. I will only let you leave under one condition."

"What is it?"

"You must promise to come back and visit me."

The two new friends smiled at each other.

"I promise."

"Very good. I, Olly, the Leo of the Zodies, will allow you to leave. Goodbye!"

"Goodbye, Olly!, said Ellen as she waved.

The little girl entered her playhouse and closed the door. She sat down on one of the bean bag chairs and closed her eyes. She did what Olly told her and thought of being home with her family. Ellen squeezed her eyes so tight, she thought they might never open again. They did, of course. When she opened her eyes, she was still in her playhouse. She knew she would be, but was her playhouse in her world or still in the land of the Zodies.

"Please let me be home," Ellen repeated as she stood and walked towards the door. Just before her hand touched the handle, she heard her father call her.

"Ellen!"

She made it home. Ellen opened the door and saw her parents and friends and other family. Some were eating cake. She had completely forgotten it was her birthday. Ellen ran to and hugged her mother and father.

"Well, little one? Do you like your gift?" asked her father.

"Yes, Daddy! Thank you so much! It's the best play-house ever!" exclaimed Ellen.

"We're glad you like it," said her mother.

Ellen was very happy to be home. Not just because it was still her birthday, but because she was home with her family. She looked back at her playhouse and saw at the bottom of the door were scratches. She knew right then two things. One: it was not a dream. Two: she was going to keep her promise and return to the land of the Zodies for more fun with Olly.

CHAPTER TWO

It had been three days since Ellen was transported to the land of the Zodies where she met Olly the Leo. She still isn't sure how she managed to last so long but now she was ready to go back. She had made a promise to Olly that she would return. Ellen also promised that she would practice her roar and she did practice very hard and very loudly and very often. Her parents felt as though they were living in the lion exhibit at the zoo.

The main reason Ellen waited so long is because she was worried her playhouse may have forgotten how to take her back to the land of the Zodies. She would wonder if the playhouse lost its magic. Ellen also wondered whether the playhouse might get lost. She hated to think about it, but because her father built it for her, what if his ability to get lost on family trips was absorbed by the playhouse.

When you are afraid something bad might happen, you may want to avoid it altogether. That's how Ellen was feeling. She would go into her playhouse but wouldn't think about Olly in case she wasn't able to see him again. But one day, she was ready to face her fears and hopefully see her friend. She had asked her mother to make two peanut butter and jelly sandwiches and once they were made, they were put inside a bag and Ellen was headed out the door.

Ellen ran into her playhouse and closed the door that still had Olly's scratch marks on it. Her father assumed that a stray cat had done it but Ellen knew better. He said he was going to fix it but Ellen said she liked it the way it was. She also didn't want her father to hurt himself again. He had only the day before had the bandages taken off his hands from when he built the playhouse.

Once Ellen was comfortable in her bean bag chair, she closed her eyes and thought of Olly and the strange world he lived in. When she opened them, things were a little blurry because she squeezed her eyes so tightly. Things came into focus again and she slowly headed for the door with her snacks in hand hoping she would be in the land of the Zodies. She opened the door and stepped outside. Standing there was Olly.

"Ellen, you came back! Just like a good Leo, you kept your promise."

"Olly! I said I would come back."

The two friends hugged each other very tightly. Ellen didn't want the hug to end because she was so happy to see her new friend again. While Olly was also very happy to see Ellen, something was distracting him. It was his nose. Rather, it was something his nose smelled.

"You." Sniff "Smell." Sniff "Sweet," said Olly as he sniffed his way to the bag she was carrying.

"Oh, yeah! I brought peanut butter and jelly sandwiches. My mother made them. I thought we could have a snack together," said Ellen.

"That sounds like a good idea but as Leo of the Zodies, I have a better one. We shall have a picnic lunch by the water."

Ellen was about to say that that does sound like a better idea when she remembered her last visit to the land Of the Zodies. She remembered she was introduced to two not very nice fish named Penelope and Isis Pisces at their home in a stream.

"By the water?" asked Ellen. "It won't be near the Pisces Stream will it?"

"Of course not!" assured Olly. "I wouldn't subject you to those two in two visits in a row. That would be cruel."

"Oh, good. Thank you."

"There is a lake not far from here. We can have our lunch there," said Olly.

With that, the two started walking. Olly asked a total of five times if it would be better if he held the bag with the sandwiches. Ellen told him five times that it would not be better because if he did, the bag would be empty by time they arrived at the lake. As I told you in the previous chapter, Ellen is a very smart girl. Along the way Ellen showed Olly how her roar was improving. Olly agreed it was improving but still needed work.

After a short walk, they were at the lake. Olly said to pick out a nice spot to eat and to be proud that he allowed her to choose. Ellen was. It was nice of Olly to give her that responsibility. It meant he trusted her as a Leo.

As Ellen looked around for the best place to sit and eat, she saw something that nearly made her eyes pop out her head. Sitting on a blanket eating sandwiches by the lake was a big hulking purple bull and a gentle looking ram in a green dress. Just as normal as could be, they were sitting there. The ram seemed to be talking endlessly as the bull simply nodded from time to time as he situated everything on the blanket into a specific place.

"Who are they?" asked a slightly frightened Ellen.

"Hmm?" wondered Olly. "The bull is Toby. He's the Taurus of the zodiac. The ram is his wife, Rosa. She is the Aries."

"Are they nice?" she asked.

"They sure are. But Rosa can talk for a long time without taking a breath so you need to make sure you have nothing to do later in the day before you start a conversation with her," Olly explained.

Olly walked over to the two on the blanket with Ellen right behind him.

"ROAR! Hello, Toby! Hello, Rosa!" greeted Olly.

"Good afternoon, Olly," Toby the bull said very seriously.

"Well, if it isn't Olly! How are you Olly? I bet you're doing well. You have either just had a great adventure or you are on your way to have one. That is always the case with you, Olly. Isn't it, Toby, dear? I hear you got your roar back. I am very glad to hear that. You without your roar would be like us without our horns. It just would not be the same," Rosa managed to say all together without fainting from exhaustion.

Rosa the ram of the zodiac had the ability to speak at length without participation from anyone, even the person or people she was talking to. Ellen was just witness to an example of it. She stood there with her mouth open. Olly noticed Rosa had paused for a brief second, which was un-usual for her, and decided to introduce Ellen.

"This is my friend Ellen from the human world. She's a Leo but doesn't know how to roar properly. It's an unfor-tunate flaw in her character but I've learned to deal with it."

"It is very nice to meet you, Ellen," said Toby.

"The human world, you say? I bet it is wonderful there. Did you have any trouble finding your way to our world. I sure hope not. It can be dangerous for a little girl to travel by herself. Although, if you're a Leo I'm sure you can take care of yourself. Nevertheless, you can never be too safe. As far as your roar, I'm sure you'll get the hang of it eventually. Some things take time. Don't be in a rush, Ellen. Take your time and I'm sure you'll get it right," Rosa said as if the words were fire in her mouth that she had to get out very quickly.

"Hi," was all Ellen could get out.

"Where is Betty?" asked Olly.

"Where else?" Toby said with a sigh.

"Of course. The water," said Olly remembering.

"Ellen, I am sure you are wondering who Betty is. It is very natural of you to wonder that. Betty is our daughter. She is the Capricorn of the zodiac. She's about your age in your human world years," said Rosa.

Toby stood and walked over to the waters' edge.

"Betty, it's time to get out and have something to eat," shouted Toby to the lake.

Ellen watched as all of a sudden, pink fins appeared to be swimming quickly towards land. As it got closer, two horns appeared followed by the rest of Betty's head. Ellen remembered that the Capricorn was a goat with a fish tail when she heard Betty 'baa' and dunk her head back under water. She did that several times. Her head would pop out the water, she'd go 'baa' and she'd disappear under the water again. Betty got out the water and Ellen saw that she was a regular goat but that she was wearing a pink bathing suit that looked like the body of a fish. Betty looked as though she were dressed as a fish for Halloween. Ellen thought the Land of the Zodies was a strange place.

"Goat's don't swim," whispered Ellen to Olly as Betty was dried off with a towel by her mother.

"This one does," Olly whispered back. "Betty, this is Ellen. Ellen, this is Betty the Capricorn."

"Hello, Ellen. It's nice to meet you," said Betty as she wrapped the towel around her neck.

"It's nice to meet you, too," said Ellen.

"Ellen, I do hope you'll forgive our daughter's fishy attire. She does insist on wearing this fish costume and there is absolutely nothing we can do to change her mind," said Rosa .

"I like my fish costume," Betty said proudly.

"It makes sense to me to wear a fish costume in the water," said Ellen.

"Maybe, but she wears it all the time. She never takes it off. That bathing suit is like her second skin," Toby said.

"Never?" asked Ellen.

"Never!" repeated Toby, Rosa and Betty at the same time.

"A goat has no business swimming in the first place," Toby the bull said sternly with his head held high. "A goat belongs on land, grazing and doing other goat things. The only time a goat should get wet is when it is washing itself."

"Your father is absolutely correct, Betty," agreed Rosa. "I really don't know why you insist on splashing about in the water every chance you get. You should see her at home, Olly and Ellen. If I look away while washing dishes, when I look back, there she is in the sink dunking her head under. It's not normal behavior befitting a goat."

"I don't care about normal goat behavior," said Betty. "I only care about how I feel when I'm in the water."

"How do you feel in the water, Betty?" asked Ellen.

"I feel free! I feel like I can do anything and there isn't anything or anyone to stop me. I feel focused when I'm swimming. I don't feel free or focused when I'm on dry land."

"Because swimming doesn't come natural to goats, what if something happened to you?" asked Toby.

"Your father and I worry about you in the water all the time," said Rosa.

"I am always very careful, Mother and Father. You watch me. When I jump out the water, I always look down to make sure the water is still there for me to splash down into again. That's how focused I am," explained Betty.

"You don't feel comfortable on dry land at all, Betty?" Ellen asked.

"The only time I feel comfortable on dry land is when I'm in my fish bathing suit. That is why I wear it all the time."

"Do you hear that, Mr. Toby and Mrs. Rosa?" Ellen said turning to the parents. "Your daughter loves to be in the water because it is where she's most happy. And she's happy on land when she wears her fish bathing suit. Don't you think you can allow her to swim and wear the costume since without it she would be unhappy? If she were unhappy, you would be unhappy, too."

"That is true," said Toby.

"We really don't want you to be unhappy, Betty," said Rosa.

"What do you think, Olly?" asked Toby. "Can she be a goat who swims in a fish bathing suit?"

"Let me see," said Olly as he scratched his chin with his paw. "Can you sound like a fish?"

"I can" said Betty. "Blub blub blub. But I want to baa like I always do."

"This is a dilemma," Olly said seriously. "A fish should blub. But I admire your bravery to baa. Ellen, you made some good points before. I couldn't have said it better myself. Since we're both Leo's, it's like I did say it and I agree with me. Betty, you will swim as much as you like."

Betty smiled so widely, she thought she would have to learn to swim with her mouth open.

"However, there is still the matter of your fish bathing suit," Olly continued. "It's silly for a goat to be dressed like a fish. It is silly for a goat to swim like a fish. What is even sillier is for someone not to do what truly makes them happy. I have decided. Betty the Capricorn, you may dress and swim like a fish if it pleases you. I am the Leo, now let it be so."

With Olly's decision made and Toby and Rosa realizing what mattered most was Betty's happiness, Betty was free to swim about as much as she liked. After everyone had finished eating, they watched as the goat/fish swam across the lake and back several times before Ellen and Olly felt it was time to say goodbye.

CHAPTER THREE

~~~

Attack of the Gesundheits

Don't you hate it when it happens? You're excited about something that is supposed to happen soon. You get your hopes up as you imagine what fun you will have. You can't seem to keep your mind on anything other than that special thing or event that is about to happen. It can be a trip to an amusement park, a favorite holiday or your birthday. Whatever it is, you can't wait.

Suddenly, out of nowhere, you sniffle. Then you cough. Next, of course, you have a temperature. It usually happens when you are at your most eager that life says it's time for a cold. It has been my experience that anticipation brings congestion. Congestion is when your nose gets all stuffy.

This is exactly how Ellen was feeling as she sat in the

kitchen waiting for her mother to give her some medicine. Not the okay tasting cherry medicine but the yucky tasting grape medicine. Ellen gulped down the syrup and hoped it would hurry up and work so she could go back to her playhouse. That is what she was looking forward to; going to see Olly in the Land of the Zodies.

Instead, she was sick and not allowed to go outside. It was still summer and not at all cold, so Ellen couldn't understand why she wasn't able to sit in her playhouse. She was told she had to wait until she got better before she could play again. This did not make Ellen happy. It was bad enough she was sneezing and her nose sometimes felt as though an elephant were sitting on it, but she also couldn't go and visit Olly.

Ellen thought hard and came up with an idea to get her to her playhouse which would transport her to the Land of the Zodies. She very convincingly explained to her mother that she left her favorite pillow in her playhouse that she just knew would help her feel better if she had it and that if she were allowed to get it, she would go right in and be right back very quickly and that it was important that she get it, not anyone else because only she knew where the pillow was and besides, only kids were allowed in her playhouse and she would be right back before she could get any sicker and her mother could watch from the kitchen window the whole time just to be sure.

Ellen said all that in one nasally breath. She learned the

trick from Rosa the ram who was the Aries of the zodiac during her last trip. Her mother, probably out of sheer dizziness from the tornado of words, decided to let her go very quickly to retrieve the pillow. Ellen was shocked but thankful her mother said yes. Ellen made her way as quickly as she could to the playhouse and closed the door. She sneezed twice before she opened it and saw she was in the Land of the Zodies. Olly stood just outside staring at her very seriously.

"Hi, Olly! I just came to see you to say I'm sick and can't come to see you today," said Ellen before noticing the almost angry look on Olly's face.

"What is it, Olly?" asked a worried Ellen.

"You sneezed," Olly said slowly. "I heard it before you opened the door. You sneezed twice."

"I know. I told you, I'm sick. I sneeze and my nose runs."

"Where does it go? Or does it run in place?"

"What?" asked Ellen.

"What?" asked Olly. "Never mind about your nose, the problem is your sneezing. Your sneezing will doom us all."

"What do you mean?" asked a concerned Ellen.

"Sneezing is dangerous here in the Land of the Zodies," Olly began to explain. "One sneeze is fine. Two sneezes is pushing your luck. Three sneezes and it's all over."

"Why? What happens after three sneezes?" Ellen asked listening intently.

"Gesundheits!" exclaimed Olly.

"In my world, that's what people say after somebody sneezes," said Ellen. "It's just a word."

"Not here. Gesundheits are nasty creatures that capture you if you're sick and make you better."

"That isn't nasty," said Ellen. "That's good!"

"You think so, do you?" said Olly. "Well guess what? If they catch you and you're healthy, they make you sick. They show up whenever someone sneezes three times in a row. After that, they chase you and if they catch you, you spend the rest of your life in their fortress as they make you sick, make you well again and then make you sick all over again. It will never end."

"Oh no! I don't want to spend the rest of my life like that," Ellen said as she tried to think non sneezy thoughts.

"Don't worry," assured Olly. "We should be fine as long as you do not sneeze more than twice."

"Okay. I'll try," said Ellen.

Don't you hate it when it happens? You want so very much for something not to happen. All you can seem to think about is that thing not happening. You use up all your energy to think of everything you can in the world that is not the thing you don't want to happen. It can be going to the doctor's office, seeing that aunt who pinches your cheeks or getting dressed up for family pictures. Whatever it is, you don't want it to happen.

Suddenly, out of nowhere, there's a tickle in your nose.

You feel it even though you told yourself not to. You sneeze once. You tell yourself not to sneeze a second time. Then you sneeze a second time. You tell yourself not to sneeze a third time. Then you sneeze a third time because you are hard headed and don't listen. It has been my experience that when you don't want something to happen, that thing will happen.

This is exactly how Ellen felt after she sneezed three times and stared at Olly who looked as though he were about to faint.

"Oh, no!" shouted Ellen as she wiped her nose. "What do I do?!"

"Get away from me!" shouted Olly. "I mean, we have to get away from here. The gesundheits can trace where the sneezes came from, so we have to get away from here."

The two frightened friends ran as fast as they could behind a boulder on top of a nearby hill. Olly thought it would be a good place to keep an eye on the creatures but not be seen by them. From this viewpoint Ellen got her first look at the gesundheits as a small army of them marched toward her playhouse. They were round furry orange creatures with a purple cross on their front. They looked like giant cotton balls. They had large noses, large eyes and their hair stood up like antennae picking up traces of sneezes. As they marched, they chanted. Half chanted "well well well" and others chanted "sicky sick!" Ellen was breathing heavily in and out after the run to hide behind the boulder.

"Stop breathing!" said Olly in a loud whisper. "The gesundheits will sense your sick germs in the air and then they'll find us."

"I have to breathe," said Ellen. "If I don't breathe, I'll die."

"They would love that," said Olly. Then he looked over the boulder and saw that the gesundheits were marching toward them. He grabbed Ellen's hand and the two ran down the hill toward a field of dandelions that were as tall as Ellen, with the fluffy looking tops that you can blow in the wind as wide as a beach ball. As they ran, Olly said they could hide out in the field and hope the gesundheits would pass by and eventually give up.

"How do you keep from getting caught by the gesundheits when you get sick here?" Ellen whispered to Olly as they both ducked down in the field listening for the creatures.

"When someone gets sick, they lock themselves in their house and do everything they can to get well again. If you're the kind of sick that makes you sneeze, we usually cover our heads with a pillow case, go into a closet and sneeze there so the sneeze isn't heard by the gesundheits," Olly explained.

There was a breeze and then a worry of a sneeze as a dandelion blew in Olly's face and tickled his nose. Thankfully, the sneeze never came, but an idea did to Ellen.

"Can the gesundheits get sick?" asked Ellen.

"I think so," said Olly. "Why?"

"Just then you almost sneezed when the dandelion blew in your face," said Ellen. "If we can blow some dandelions at the gesundheits, they might sneeze and start to go after each other. After that, we can run back to my playhouse and I can go home and then they won't have anyone but their own selves to want to make better."

Olly thought for a second.

"That is a brilliant idea!" he said. "That idea is so good, if it were food, I'd eat it. I would expect nothing less from a Leo in training."

With Ellen's idea given the stamp of approval from Olly, the two friends grabbed an armful of dandelions and made their way out of the field. Olly, the brave little Leo of the zodiac, picked out one from his bunch and stuffed his face in the flower and within seconds, he began to sneeze. He sneezed once. Then he sneezed a second time. And yes, thankfully, he sneezed a third time. Immediately, they heard the marching and chanting of the gesundheits getting closer. The two friends were scared. If this idea didn't work, they didn't know what they would do.

The gesundheits appeared before them as Ellen and Olly did their very best to look brave. When the creatures stopped their marching about five feet away, one gesundheit came forward and stood before Olly. Olly and Ellen looked at each other, nodded and took in a deep breath. Then they blew one of the dandelions in the face of the lone gesundheit. The creature shook his head several times and its eyes became very big as it realized a sneeze was on its way out.

AATCHOO!!

Two more sneezes followed.

AATCHOO!! AATCHOO!!

I wish I could describe for you the look of panic on the gesundheits face as it turned slowly around to face its own kind and realized they would be coming for him. The other gesundheits were confused yet determined as they marched towards their sneezing relation. With wobbly legs, Olly and Ellen stood where they were as the creatures got closer. Once the gesundheits were about to overtake them and the lone sneezing gesundheit, Ellen and Olly blew all the dandelions in their arms in the direction of the creatures who instantly started a loud chorus of sneezes.

AATCHOO!!   AATCHOO!!   AATCHOO!! AATCHOO!!

As the utterly confused gesundheits were stuck in their sneezing fits, Olly and Ellen ran as fast as their legs could go and made it to Ellen's playhouse.

"You better go home and get better," said an out of breath Olly. "Do not come back until you are one billion percent healthy. That is an order."

"Yes, sir!" responded an out of breath Ellen.

Ellen walked into her playhouse and was transported back to the human world. She almost walked out without her pillow that she told her mother she went in to get. She grabbed it and walked toward her house. Her mother was smiling as she watched from the window like she said she would. Once inside, she was told to go to her room and rest. Her mother said it would help the medicine to work. Ellen was just about to drift off to sleep when she suddenly sneezed.

AATCHOO!

She knew in her world she was safe.

"Gesundheit!" shouted her father from downstairs. Ellen jumped up.

"WHERE?!" she shouted.

CHAPTER FOUR

Five W's and an H

O ne day in the land of the Zodies, Olly and Ellen were sitting under a tree thinking about what would be the proper thing to think about while sitting under a tree. Olly said he thought they should think about trees because they were right there and it would be rude not to give a thought to them. Ellen said they should look up at the sky and figure out what the clouds were trying to look like today. It seems clouds don't much like being clouds because they always look like things other than clouds. Olly felt this way also and told Ellen. She agreed.

As the two friends were gazing up at the sky, they all of a sudden heard two voices call out.

"There you are!" said the female voice. "We found you!"

"Oh, no," said Olly, recognizing the voice instantly. Ellen looked in the direction the voice came from and appearing just over the hill, all she saw was a giant eyeball. Ellen's eyes became quite big as she looked at the rest of the eyeball as it came closer. The eyeball was attached to the top of a big hand that walked on its fingers. On the middle finger, was a large ring with a red gem.

"Who is that?!" asked Ellen as she stared in wonder.

"They are Jim and Jenny Gemini," explained Olly. "They're the Gemini twins of the Zodiac. Jim is the eye and the gem is Jenny."

Jim and jenny were now standing before Ellen and Olly. Ellen couldn't help but notice that Jim and Jenny did not look alike. Not even a little. She did not want to be rude so she whispered her observation to Olly. He whispered back simply that things were different in this world.

"Good afternoon, Olly and Ellen," said Jenny. Ellen noticed that the gem glowed whenever Jenny spoke.

"Good afternoon Ellen and Olly," said Jim. When he spoke, his eyelid would open and close which meant it was closed when not speaking.

"It figures you two would already know about Ellen," said Olly. Ellen did realize the twins knew her name before she was introduced.

"Ellen, these two are junior reporters here," said Olly. "They collect information, most of the time it's true, and spread it to everyone in the land of the Zodies."

"That is right," said Jenny. "We take it upon ourselves to inform our precious world of all that happens. It is important to know what is going on around you."

"We believe being informed is a right," added Jim. "It is my sister's and my privilege to be the ones to supply that information."

"Currently, Ellen, you interest us a great deal and we believe the citizens of the Land of the Zodies have a right to know more about you," said Jenny as her gem glowed with every word.

"I am sure you wouldn't mind answering a few questions about yourself so we can spread the word that you mean us no harm," said Jim as his eye opened and closed with each word.

Ellen looked at Olly for help. He turned to her and whispered in her ear.

"They won't hurt you," he whispered. "The worst they'll do is say something bad about you to people. But if you answer their questions honestly, you have nothing to worry about."

"Really?" asked Ellen.

"Oh, if you lie, you will be trapped in a box for eternity," Olly continued. "Eternity means forever."

"Is Olly telling you about the box you will be trapped in forever if you do not tell the truth?" asked Jim.

"What box?" asked a frightened Ellen.

"During our questioning, your body will be separated

into different boxes," explained Jenny. "Every time you answer a question honestly, a part of your body will be set free. If you answer all questions dishonestly, you will be trapped in box for the rest of your life."

"It is a strange way to get the truth, but we find it is the best way," said Jim.

"Shall we get started?" asked Jenny.

Ellen looked at Olly once more and he told her to stay calm and to tell the truth. Then she turned to the twins.

"Okay, I'm ready," she said bravely. "I don't want the people of the land of the Zodies to believe anything but the truth about me. So box me and ask me!"

At that moment, Olly felt very proud that Ellen was a Leo, even if she couldn't roar very well yet. Jim and Jenny were impressed as well. The twins stepped close to Ellen and she did her best to stand strong. Suddenly, Jenny began to shout.

"ONE, TWO, THREE, FOUR, FIVE W's!" she shouted.

Then, before Ellen knew it, she saw that each arm, each leg and her body from neck to waist, was inside of its own box that had the letter 'W' on it.

"ONE H!" shouted Jim.

Now Ellen's head was inside of a box. Even though this box was see through, she could see an 'H' on it. Ellen thought she couldn't get more scared than she was now.

"Apart!" shouted the twins together. Then each of the six boxes with a different part of Ellen's body, went into different directions. Ellen felt no pain but couldn't believe she was staring at her body parts floating around in the air.

"Time for the first question," said Jenny. "Who are you?"

"I am Ellen Campbell."

"Question two," said Jim. "What brings you to the land of the Zodies?"

"My playhouse brings me here."

"Question three," said Jenny. "Where did you come from?"

"I came from the human world."

Ellen knew she was answering honestly, but she couldn't help but look at each box that contained part of her body to see if it might disappear.

"Question four," said Jim. "When did you first begin to travel to here?"

Ellen began to be very concerned for her body because she did not know how long she had been coming to the land of the Zodies. She looked at Olly.

"Just be honest!" Olly shouted.

"I don't know when I first came here," Ellen said. "I really don't remember."

"Question five," said Jenny. "Why do you keep coming back to the land of the Zodies?"

"Because this is where Olly is and Olly is my best friend," answered Ellen. "I have fun here, especially when I meet new people."

"This is the last question," said Jim. "Question six: how come you don't stay in the land of the Zodies?"

"I like it here very much," Ellen began honestly. "I like everyone that I have met here, except the Pisces sisters. But if I stayed here, I would miss my parents and my parents would miss me. I would be very sad if I never say my mother and father again. I like having fun here, but I need to go home again when the fun is over."

After a short pause that to Ellen seemed to last a very long time, the gem glowed.

"We have determined, Ellen, that you have answered our questions honestly," said Jenny.

"You are free to go," said Jim.

Just then, the six boxes came together, only not in the right order. Ellen had a leg where her head should be and her head was where an arm should have been. The boxes rearranged themselves and when everything was in its proper place, the boxes disappeared. Ellen was very happy to be back on the ground in and in one piece. Olly ran to her and the friends hugged each other tightly.

"We will spread the good word about you to everyone in the land of the Zodies," said Jenny.

"Thank you for your cooperation," said Jim.

"You're welcome," said a relieved Ellen.

CHAPTER FiVE

lly and Ellen were taking a walk in the land of the Zodies one day when a thought suddenly roared into Olly's head. Normally ideas pop into people's heads but this one roared into Olly's. The thought was that he should go and visit Mr. Fincher. Mr. Fincher, Olly explained, was the Cancer of the zodiac. Ellen remembered that the cancer was a crab and became very excited to meet another member of the zodiac. She then became a little nervous as she remembered being stuck in boxes by the Gemini twins.

As they walked towards his house, Ellen noticed the

weather begin to change. They left a grass covered land and in just a few steps, were on land that looked like a beach. There was a long metal tube that sat between two palm trees that started outside the sand covered ground and disappeared underneath it. The beginning part had a door that when they were in front of, Olly knocked.

The door opened and Olly and Ellen crawled in. They hadn't crawled far when there was another door before them. Olly knocked on this one and a grumpy sounding voice answered.

"Who is it?" said Mr. Fincher.

Olly roared and on the other side of the door Mr. Fincher groaned. There was a pause and then the circular door opened. Ellen was now staring at Mr. Fincher the red crab. He stood on four legs, two on each side. Four arms stayed folded across his chest while two large claws were resting on his hips. He welcomed them both into his home of sand walls, floor and ceiling. The inside was big enough for them to stand up straight in.

"It is just my luck to get a visit from you, Olly, at a time like this," said Mr. Fincher as one eye looked at Olly and the other at Ellen. Ellen tried not to stare at the crabs eyes that were only connected to his body by a thin vein.

"What have you come to pester me about today?" he said as now both eyes were focused on Ellen.

"Whatever it is, you have brought a friend, or perhaps an enemy, to assist you."

"This is Ellen, and she is my friend," said Olly.

"Ah, yes," said Mr. Fincher. "The Gemini twins wrote about you in the Land of the Zodies Daily newspaper."

Ellen had no idea that her answers to the twins questions would end up in a newspaper. She wondered if this meant she was famous. Or maybe that other word that was similar to it she heard once. "Was it infamous?" she wondered to herself.

"The article said you were an honest girl who means no harm, but I am not entirely convinced if you don't mind my saying so," said the crab. "But as you are a friend of Olly, I suppose I'll be nice."

Ellen did mind but she was more interested in what he said earlier.

"What did you mean when you said at a time like this?" she asked.

"I meant at a time when I have lost something so very important," Mr. Fincher said looking and sounding concerned.

"What is it?" asked Olly.

"I cannot find my jar of remembers," said Mr. Fincher.

Ellen didn't know what that was but she felt sad for him. Olly laughed very loudly.

"What is a jar of remembers?" Ellen asked.

"It's-It's," Olly tried to explain but laughter kept getting in the way.

"My jar of remembers is a jar I keep filled with things I

want or need to remember and I go through it every morning," Mr. Fincher was able to explain.

"And-and," Olly tried to continue but more laughter got in the way.

"I usually keep it in a specific place, which is on my bookcase, but I looked and it isn't there," said Mr. Fincher.

"And now he can't remember where he put it!!" Olly managed to say through laughter.

"That isn't even the worst part of the story," Mr. Fincher was able to say above Olly's laughing. "I do remember writing a purple note and placing it in my jar before I went to bed and woke up this morning and couldn't remember its location."

"What does a purple note mean?" asked Ellen.

"Mr. Fincher writes ordinary things he needs to remember on white paper. He writes very important things he needs to remember on purple paper with yellow circles," said Olly as he finally calmed down.

"That is correct," said the worried crab. "I have to find my jar so I can find out what it is I must remember."

"We'll help you look for it, won't we, Olly?" said Ellen.

"Of course, we will!" answered Olly.

"That would be such a help," said Mr. Fincher, who even though was truly thankful, always said things in a begrudging way. "Thank you."

As the three of them began to look around Mr. Fincher's home for his jar of remembers, he said what sometimes helps him is hearing other peoples' remembrances. With that, they each went down a list of things they remember while continuing to look.

Olly remembered the peanut butter and jelly sandwich Ellen shared with him once. He remembered when he lost his roar and found that a worm was using it. Olly also remembered when he and Ellen went up against the gesundheits. He remembered the peanut butter and jelly sandwich again. Then he remembered when he first met Ellen and they became friends.

Ellen remembered the gesundheits as well. She also remembered meeting the Pisces sisters and not liking them very much. She remembered being scared when she was questioned by the Gemini twins. Ellen especially remembered meeting Olly for the first time.

Mr. Fincher remembered what he had for breakfast fifty-seven years ago. He remembered getting into a kerfuffle with S.C. Orp, who was the scorpion of the zodiac, over whose claws were bigger. He remembered every book he has read and was going to name each one when Olly said they would leave immediately if he didn't stop. Mr. Fincher remembered that Olly always means what he says so he stopped.

As Mr. Fincher was searching underneath his sofa and Olly was looking in the refrigerator, Ellen was on the floor in a closet. She moved a mop, a broom and lifted up an upside down bucket and gave a shout.

"I think I found it! I think I found it!" she exclaimed.

Mr. Fincher and Olly came running and Ellen turned to them holding a clear jar full of small rolled up pieces of paper. All but one of the pieces of paper was white. One was purple with yellow circles.

"That's it! You really found it!" shouted Mr. Fincher as he snapped his red claws again and again in excitement. "Thank you so much, Ellen!"

"You're welcome," Ellen said.

Before Mr. Fincher opened the jar, he looked again at Ellen.

"I suppose you aren't all that bad for a human," he said.

"Thank you," she said.

Mr. Fincher walked to his table and set the jar down. Slowly, he opened it and removed the rolled up yellow spotted purple piece of paper. When he unrolled it, he read what it said. Olly and Ellen were very anxious to hear what this important remember was. They leaned in close and listened.

"You have moved your jar of remembers to its new place in the closet under the bucket" read Mr. Fincher.

Ellen just smiled. Olly just fainted.

CHAPTER SIX

Good Maiden, Bad Maiden

s always, Ellen was greeted by Olly when she stepped out of her playhouse and into the Land of the Zodies. The two friends hugged each other extra tightly because it had been a while since Ellen had visited Olly. The reason for her absence was a visiting aunt and grandmother who occupied most of Ellen's time. She wanted very badly to see Olly but she loved the time she spent with her family.

It was decided by Olly, as most things are, that in order to catch up on what the other was doing during their time apart, a walk was the best use of their time. He said during a walk is the best time to talk. When they told each other everything the other missed, Ellen looked up and noticed they were walking past a house that shone such a pretty shiny blue that it almost glowed. To Ellen it looked a bit like those houses people keep plants and flowers in. A greenhouse, Ellen thought it was called. It looked as though it were made of glass or ice.

Olly told her this is where Virginia the Virgo of the zodiac lived. Ellen asked if she were a nice person because she wanted to meet the Virgo. Olly told Ellen that there was no one in all the land of the Zodies who was as nice and kind as the maiden Virginia the Virgo. Ellen was very happy to hear that. The two walked up the three steps to the front door and knocked. After a brief moment, the door opened and there stood a tall, beautiful woman who was completely blue from head to toe. Ellen assumed she had toes because she couldn't see them due to the long gown she wore. When she walked, it looked like she floated. Her blue hair flowed down to her waist. When she spoke, it was the sweetest sounding sound Ellen ever heard. You could tell she was a very nice person.

"Hello, Olilio," said Virginia as she bent down to look him in the eyes. "It is so very nice to see you. Hello to you, as well, Ellen."

Ellen blushed at the woman knowing her name. She was also surprised that she called Olly by his whole first name. Olly must respect her a lot if she could get away with it. Virginia then welcomed them into her home.

"Hello, Virginia," said Olly. "You've already heard about Ellen but she hasn't met you, so here she is to meet you."

"It's nice to meet you Virginia," said Ellen.

"It is nice to meet you as well, Ellen," said Virginia before she motioned for them to sit down. "Please forgive me if I appear frazzled at the moment."

Ellen and Olly looked at the maiden and then each other. She appeared to them to be the most unfrazzled person of all time. She looked completely calm. Ellen looked around the house and saw that everything looked perfect. Everything was tidy and perfect. Olly thought the same thing because he told Virginia so after he said she was crazy for thinking she looked frazzled.

"I am having some difficulty with myself right now," Virginia explained. "In fact, you just proved a point I've been making to myself. I am perfect!"

"Why is that a bad thing?" asked a confused Ellen.

"I am not at all sure that I want to be perfect," Virginia said. "I have realized that everyone sees me as perfect, calm and collected. You only just met me, Ellen. Did you think those nice things about me instantly?"

"Yes," Ellen answered honestly.

"Exactly!" the maiden exclaimed although even her shout sounded calm and peaceful. "I want to be more than what people always expect of me. I want to know if there is more to me than this pristine exterior."

"I'm sorry, Virginia, but I think you should be happy to be seen as all those good things by people," said Ellen standing. "Being good is good. It isn't something to feel bad about. It isn't something you should change. You should stay the way you are."

Virginia was just about to say that Ellen was right and she should be proud with being a sweet, kind person when Olly jumped up and roared.

RRROAARR!!

"Don't stay," he said. "Change the way you are."

"What do you mean, Olilio?" asked Virginia.

"Virginia, you want to be bad so badly, then be bad. Don't just want to know if you could or should, just be it. Good is what you are. Bad is what you want to be. Try it out! Don't be so perfect. Don't be so kind."

Ellen could not believe what she was hearing Olly say. I'm a little shocked myself. Olly, however, was very sure of what he was saying. Virginia began to think about Olly's suggestion to just try out acting differently than she normally does when she isn't even trying. She decided.

"For one day," Virginia started. "For one day, I will act in the opposite way that I normally do. I will search myself for a more unpredictable way of being. Thank you, Olly."

Olly suggested as a way to get started, they begin right then by messing up her home. He said everything is so neat and tidy and should be messed up. He grabbed pillows and threw them in the air. He told Virginia to knock over a chair. This was her first try so she picked up the chair slowly and carefully placed it on its side on the floor. Even though she disagreed, Ellen wanted to join in so she flipped a rug so it was in a clump in a corner.

When they were done, Virginia looked around her once lovely home at the mess it now was. She hid very well from Olly and Ellen the horror she was feeling at the state of the place. Olly said next, Virginia needs to try out her new bad behavior on others. The maiden reluctantly agreed and the three of them left her house and looked for victims as Olly called them. Secretly, Virginia was happy to not have to look at her ransacked home.

They made their way to the lake that Ellen met Toby, Rosa and Betty. In the lake swimming was Betty.

"Call Betty over and try out being nasty," said Olly. "If nasty is how you want to be, now is an opportunity."

With that, Olly grabbed Ellen's hand and pulled her behind a tree. They popped their heads from behind the tree so they could watch.

"Betty! Come here a second won't you?" shouted Virginia.

Betty looked up and saw the maiden. She knew the maiden was someone who always encouraged her swimming even though she was a goat. She swam quickly and met Virginia on land.

"Hello, Virginia," said the young goat as she stood dripping in her fish bathing suit.

Virginia thought the best way was to say something nasty and run away quickly.

"You do know it's stupid for a goat to go around swimming in a fish suit, right? You will never be as good as a real fish so you should just stop fooling yourself" she said with all the strength she could gather before running away but not before she saw tears form in the little goats eyes.

Olly and Ellen ran after her and found her with tears in her eyes.

"That was horrible," Virginia said trying not to cry. "I just hurt that poor girl's feelings. I feel terrible."

"Terrible is the opposite of what you normally are so you need to get used to it," said Olly rather coldly.

Virginia dried her tears and again the three of them were off looking for another chance for her to not be so perfect. They found that chance in the form of a rolled up purple piece of paper with yellow circles on it stuck in a bush they walked by. Ellen recognized the paper as an important remember note from Mr. Fincher's jar of remembers.

Coming towards them looking up in trees and on the ground was Mr. Fincher. Olly told Virginia to stand in front of the bush to hide the note and if asked, to say she has not seen it. Again he and Ellen hid as a concerned Mr. Fincher approached the maiden. Mr. Fincher knew the maiden would help him find his remember note.

"Virginia, it is awful," said the crab. "This morning was such a lovely morning that I decided to leave my doors open to let the breeze in. I then thought I would wash my jar of remembers so I emptied it on the table when a gust of wind carried my remember notes all over the house. I thought I had retrieved them all when one flew right out the doors and in this direction. As you can see, I am in quite a state. Have you by chance seen a rolled up piece of purple paper with yellow circles on it?"

Virginia bit her lip and kept shaking her head no so fast, it looked to Ellen like it would go flying into the air like a helicopter any second. Mr. Fincher the crab knew that even though she said nothing, Virginia would say something if she knew something so he said goodbye and scurried away looking for his remember note. As soon as Mr. Fincher was gone, Olly and Ellen came out of hiding.

"Well, you've had some experience being the opposite of how you normally are," said Olly. "Are you ready to make being mean and imperfect your new way of life?"

"Absolutely not!" said Virginia as she wiped tears from her eyes. "I never want to be this way again. Not for one more second. It is a terrible way live if it means treating people the way I have. Helping people is good. Being kind to people is good. Not being messy is good. I am good and I love being that way!"

"Yeah! You should," said Ellen.

"I'm glad you learned your lesson," said Olly. "You are perfect the way you are and nothing about you should be changed."

"That's right," said Ellen.

"Thank you both," said Virginia.

"I felt like you needed to see what it's like to be nasty to know you wouldn't want to be nasty," said Olly. "Of course I was right and I knew I would be."

"Thank you both again but if you will excuse me, I need to go right some terrible wrongs," Virginia said, as she dried her eyes. "While I'm busy doing that, can you both do me a favor?"

"Sure. What is it?" asked Ellen.

"Can you please go back to my house and clean up the mess we made?" Virginia said instantly.

CHAPTER SEVEN

S.C. Orp

Olly and Ellen had just finished having a fun game of hide and seek with Betty the goat. Olly was able to find the two girls easily three times in a row because of his superior sense of smell he kept telling them. His explanation for why he kept getting found every other time was that he let them win because he felt bad for winning so often.

They were headed to Ellen's playhouse so she could go back to her world. As they got closer, they noticed the play-house was gone. They ran as fast as they could to its normal spot and gone it was. They both wondered if the wind might have blown it away but as there wasn't any strong wind blowing, it couldn't have been that they decided. Ellen wondered if her playhouse could move on its own. It could transport her between two worlds, why couldn't it move on its own, she thought.

Ellen and Olly looked around the area for clues when Olly noticed moving slowly and bumpily down the hill was Ellen's playhouse. They ran to get a closer look and saw the playhouse sitting on top of a scorpion about as big as the playhouse that was crawling away as fast as it could. The scorpion's tail held tight to the top of the playhouse.

"That's Mr. Orp," said Olly recognizing the thief. "S.C. Orp is the Scorpio of the zodiac. He's more of a crab than Mr. Fincher."

"What should we do?" asked Ellen watching as her only way home got further away from her.

"He's has your playhouse. It doesn't belong to him. Don't be silly! We're going to get back your playhouse!" said Olly.

With that decided, they ran after the scorpion. As they got closer, S.C. Orp heard their approaching footsteps and he tried to crawl even faster which I don't need to tell you smart readers was quite difficult for him as he had a playhouse on his back. Still, he managed to keep ahead of them. Olly and Ellen weren't slowing down. Mr. Orp crawled all the way to his home which was underneath a large white rock. Ellen and Olly were right behind him.

"Listen up, Orp!" said Olly when the chase ended. "I don't know why you took Ellen's playhouse, but I know you better give it back."

Mr. Orp turned around and faced the two angry friends.

"Don't you think I need it more than she does?" Mr. Orp asked.

"How can you need it more than me when it belongs to me?" asked Ellen though she wasn't really sure where to look because there was no sign of a face on S.C. Orp.

"Isn't that a good question, Olly?" asked Orp. "Don't you agree you asked a good question, Ellen?"

"I want my playhouse back, Mr. Orp," pleaded Ellen.

"Do you want it so you can go back home?" asked the scorpion.

"Yes, sir."

"Isn't that sweet? Wouldn't it be sweet if I gave you your playhouse back? Well, I won't. I want it and it's staying here!" shouted Orp.

"Tell me why you need it?" asked Ellen again.

"Are you asking me another question?" asked Orp as he set the playhouse down beside him. "Are you challenging me?"

"Here it comes," said Olly.

"I'm not challenging you, Mr. Orp," said Ellen.

"Isn't it very wise of her not to, Olly?" asked Orp. "You should know that I am the land of the Zodies champion questioner thirty years straight. No one anywhere can ask more questions than me. I can ask hundreds of questions on any topic. I once beat the Queen Questionmark of Newquestionland in a question off. My record is five hundred questions asked in a row."

"How about you just answer her question?" asked an annoyed Olly. "What do you need her playhouse for?"

"I read about Ellen and her magical playhouse in the story by the Gemini twins. It seems she can travel between our world and her human world through the playhouse. As you know very well Olly, I cannot stand having visitors as I feel that they want to spy on my special top secret projects and experiments that will revolutionize the world. I crave the utmost privacy. I feel, Ellen, that if I used your playhouse as my front door, whenever unwanted visitors walked in, they would be transported far away to your human world and cease to be a nuisance," explained S.C. Orp.

"I have an idea," said Ellen after thinking for a moment. "If you promise to give me back my playhouse, I promise I will make up a sign that will keep anyone away."

"A sign?!" exclaimed Orp. "I have tried them all. Keep out! No soliciting! Beware of dog! I'm a scorpion and will sting you! Nothing works."

"This sign will," said Ellen confidently. "If you have a piece of board and a marker, I'll make it for you to put up right away."

S.C. Orp crawled underneath his rock and returned a minute later holding a white piece of cardboard in one claw and a black marker in the other. He handed them to Ellen who started scribbling right away. When she finished writing, she handed the sign to Mr. Orp who read it aloud.

"Only knock if you can answer five hundred questions

on any subject," read Mr. Orp as he smiled. Ellen was sure she saw him smile.

After Mr. Orp put the sign up on his rock, he placed the playhouse on his back and he, Ellen and Olly made their way back to the playhouse's original location.

CHAPTER EIGHT

The No Time Loser

ven after all her visits, Ellen still had butterflies in her stomach right before she opened the door of her playhouse to enter the land of the Zodies. As always, Olly greeted her with a big smile because he was always happy to see her come back. Before she left for her world the last time she was with Olly, he told Ellen to bring a winter coat because he would be taking her to Winter Town. Ellen had never been there but she remembered seeing it from far away when she first came to the land of the Zodies.

In Ellen's world, it was still warm outside so she had a difficult time explaining to her parents why she was carrying her heavy winter coat to play in her playhouse. Ellen did her best to explain by saying things like there may be another polar vortex. She had heard her parents talking about a polar vortex earlier in the year. She also mentioned global warming and an ice age may cause the weather to become very cold at any minute and she wanted to be ready in case it did. Ellen was very smart and so were her parents because they thought it wise to not ask any further questions and just let her go on her way.

Here she was back in the land of the Zodies and she and Olly were just entering Winter Town. With just one step, the two friends went from walking on grass to walking on six inches of snow. The cold white stuff covered trees and mountains all around them. Ellen thankfully not only remembered her coat but also to wear long pants. She had forgotten, however, her boots. She would not make that mistake again.

Olly and Ellen ran about and played in the snow. They made snow angels. I am sorry. Ellen made snow angels. Olly made snow Leos. After they made an attempt at making a snowman, they decided there was only one thing left to do and that was to have a snowball fight. At one point, Olly slipped and slid down a hill. Ellen laughed then ran and laughed at the same time after Olly to make sure he was all right. She looked up in time to see Olly just as he was about to slam into the strangest thing she had seen since she came to the land of the Zodies. It was a centaur.

Ellen stared at the creature which from the waist up

looked like a human man and from the waist down, had the body of a dark brown horse. He was taking aim with a bow and arrow at a scratched in target on a tree just as Olly plowed into its back legs from the side. The arrow went flying high into the air and Ellen hoped the centaur wouldn't be angry Olly made him miss. He would not be angry because he did not miss. The arrow flew into the air and looked as though it would land in a snow covered bush but instead suddenly changed course and landed dead in the center of the target.

Olly got to his feet as the centaur turned around and looked down at him.

"My, if it isn't Olly!" said the centaur. "Bumping into my back legs is indeed an interesting way of saying hello yet is not the strangest entrance you have made. How do you fare today?"

"RROAARR!" roared Olly with a smile.

"Very glad to hear it," said the centaur.

"Are you okay, Olly?" asked Ellen walking up and seeing that the centaur was safe to approach.

"Ellen, this is Arnold," introduced Olly. "He's the Sagittarius of the zodiac."

"Hello, Arnold," said Ellen as she tried not to stare at his waist where the horse part of his body began.

"It is a privilege to meet you, Ellen," said Arnold, offering his hand to shake.

"I didn't know you had returned," said Olly. "Arnold is

always traveling to distant lands. Whenever you see him, he is either on his way or has just come back from somewhere exciting."

"This is indeed true. I only just returned home yesterday and I am deeply disappointed to say I again was not successful," said Arnold with great sadness.

"What happened?" asked Ellen hearing the sadness in Arnold's voice. "Or what didn't happen?"

"I am not a failure," said Arnold as if this was a terrible thing to admit. "I am an archer. I live and breathe only to pull an arrow from my quiver and release it at my intended target. No matter what the circumstances, however, I always end up making a perfect shot. I absolutely never miss. Just watch."

Arnold slowly pulled an arrow from his quiver of arrows that was strapped to his back. He positioned it in his bow and pointed it above him. He let the arrow fly and they all watched as the arrow flew high into the air, straight above them then flipped upside down and headed right for the target on the tree where it split it half the first arrow he shot there.

"Ellen of the human world, do not judge me but this is my curse," Arnold said spiritlessly. "I am lucky."

To prove how lucky he was and how awful he felt about it, Arnold showcased several more times his inability to lose. He aimed his bow and arrows in every direction except towards the target on the tree and each time the arrow made its way to the target. At one point, Ellen thought she would faint because Arnold took aim at himself but again the arrow twisted and found the target on the tree.

"It is not only in archery that I cannot fail," Arnold said. "Olly, make a snowball and throw it at me, if you do not mind."

In a second, Olly dropped to his knees and was making a snowball. When he patted it twice, he put some distance between himself and Arnold. Then he hurled the ball at Arnold but the snowball looped around and hit Olly in the face. I do not want you to think Olly is stupid because he is definitely not. The reason Olly made another snowball immediately is because his pride could not stand the embarrassment. Not stupidity. Again the snowball looped and hit Olly right in the face. Both times Ellen laughed. Arnold did not. He only became more dejected.

It began to snow and Arnold said he left his umbrella at his home right by the door. With the snow as a possible obstacle, he decided to try another shot. Instead of an arrow, he pulled an umbrella from his quiver. They all knew it wasn't there before.

"Of course," said Arnold. "This is precisely why I travel all over the land. I am in desperate search for something to fail at. I have searched endlessly for an opportunity to fail. Lessons are learned when mistakes are made. If one is always right, they do not rise to a higher level of understanding. However, if one fails, they learn why they failed, how to redeem themselves and how not to make the same mistake again. The great lesson of failure has eluded me my whole life and I grow impatient waiting for it."

"If you've been searching for a long time for something to fail at, and you haven't found it then you failed at finding something that happens to everyone else all the time," said Ellen.

Arnold thought about this. Ever since he could remember, he was lucky. Everything always turned out well for him and he never tried hard for it to. His whole life was one long lucky streak. Everyday people make mistakes and learn from them while he felt he had to go on journeys to find what he could fail at and it turns out every single one of his journeys was an example of failure. Arnold had never been so happy.

"I AM A FAILURE!!" shouted Arnold as he stood on his hind legs and raising his front ones high into the air and kicking them about.

After saying their goodbyes, Olly and Ellen started to head back to her playhouse. When they got near a tree, Olly whispered for Ellen to hide and the two hid behind the tree. Olly said he was determined to hit Arnold who went back to practicing his archery. He gathered some snow and shaped it into a ball. Olly took aim and threw the snowball which looped around and hit him in the face causing him to fall back against the tree which shook loose the snow that came down and buried Olly. Ellen spent the next five minutes laughing and digging Olly out from underneath the pile of snow.

CHAPTER NINE

Harrius the Aquarius

One day Olly and Ellen were walking to nowhere in particular in the land of the Zodies. Sometimes when she came to the land of the Zodies, Olly would have some special place he wanted to show Ellen or someone special to visit or they would just by chance have something exciting to do. This time, they simply decided to go for a walk. They had gone on walks before but this walk was different from those others. Something happened on this walk that had never happened before.

What happened on this walk happens to the best of friendships. Ellen and Olly had a fight. I know. I was as surprised as you are. It all started with a simple question. Simple causes often have complicated effects. When Ellen asked her question, she never thought it would lead to her fighting with her best friend.

"Your name is Olilio N. Lion," said Ellen as she and Olly walked down a hill. "What does the 'n' stand for?"

"Never you mind what it stands for," responded Olly with a growl. "Olly is what I like to be called so Olly is all that matters."

"I just wondered what the 'n' stood for. You never told me."

"I know I never told you," Olly said. "If I wanted you to know, I would have told by now."

"Am I not allowed to know because I'm not a member of the zodiac?" asked Ellen.

"No, that isn't it," answered Olly as he began to walk a little faster than Ellen as if trying to outrun her questions.

"Do the other Zodies know your middle name?"

"Yes."

"Am I not allowed to know because my roar isn't perfect yet?"

"No, that isn't it either."

"Is it because I'm human?" asked Ellen, trying to keep up with Olly.

"No."

"Why won't you tell me what your middle name is, Olly?"

Olly said nothing.

"Why can't I know what it is?"

Again Olly did not respond.

"I thought we were friends. You know my middle name is Wanda. It was my grandmother's first name."

Olly kept on walking and not answering Ellen.

"Fine! If you won't talk to me, I won't talk to you either!" shouted Ellen.

Just like that, the two friends stopped speaking to one another. The two kept walking down the hill but with Olly on one side and Ellen on the other. They wouldn't even look in the others direction. Ellen was so angry, she would have gone off on her own had she known where she was or how to get back to her playhouse. That is the same reason Olly didn't walk too far ahead of her.

A middle name had caused two very close friends to want to no longer speak. No matter what causes a fight between two people who care about each other, it hurts them both to not be together. Olly felt the same pain Ellen felt in her chest. It wasn't an 'ow' kind of pain. It was an 'I don't want to be fighting with my friend' kind of pain. Unfortunately, even with this pain, they were both determined not to speak before the other one did first.

As they continued stomping down the hill (they ceased walking a while back), they heard a sound of something hitting the ground getting closer. Olly and Ellen turned at the same time, avoiding looking at each other, to see what was heading towards them. At the top of the hill hopped a jar half the size of Ellen. As it hopped towards the two silent friends, Ellen could see on each side of the jar were handles that someone inside the jar was gripping tightly with both hands and water splashing about with every hop. The jar was green at the bottom and gold at the top.

"Hello, Harrius!" said Olly when the jar came to a stop.

Ellen looked at the jar and saw nothing but two large eyeballs and wild blue hair.

"Hello, Olly," said Harrius. "You must be Ellen. I'm sorry, but I can't stay and chat. I'm off to the library to return this book."

Harrius reached into his jar and pulled out a book soaked cover to cover. He then put it back with a splash.

"There's a library here?" asked Ellen.

"Of course there is!" said Harrius.

"I guess that's something else I don't know," said Ellen while trying to look at Olly without looking at him the way you do when you're angry with someone.

"Do you know what, Harrius?" asked Olly. "You are the perfect person for this situation."

"What situation is that?" asked Harrius, though he would have preferred not to involve himself.

"Ellen can't seem to understand that I just do not want to tell her my middle name. Can you use your powers to make her accept it so we can be friends again?"

"First of all, Olly, I cannot guarantee that Ellen will see things the way you want her to. My powers don't work that way. Secondly, Ellen has to decide on her own if she wants to try it. No one can force her," explained Harrius.

After Ellen asked what they were talking about, Harrius explained that if someone looks into his jar, they will see reflected back at them the point of view of someone in that persons' life. It will help them see an opinion that is not their own.

"I will if you will," said Ellen to Olly when she was sure she understood.

"I don't mean to rush the two of you, but I must get to the library before it closes," said Harrius as his jar shook with the fear that he might have another overdue book.

Ellen decided to go first. Harrius told her to simply look into his jar. When Ellen looked down past the blue hair, she saw her reflection. Instantly, her reflection changed and she saw Olly's face where hers should be. When she blinked, he did. When she made funny faces, he made the exact same ones. Then she heard a voice in her head that sounded like Olly.

"I don't want Ellen to know my middle name because it is embarrassing and even though she is my friend, I feel like she won't think I'm worth being friends with anymore because my middle name is so silly. Also, I think it is my right to not say what my middle name is. I shouldn't lose a friend over that," said Olly in Ellen's mind.

Suddenly, Ellen saw herself in the water and stood up straight. Now it was Olly's turn. Olly bent over Harrius's jar and at first saw himself before his reflection changed to Ellen's. Then he heard Ellen's voice in his head.

"Olly is the best friend I have ever had and because of that, I don't like that he has a secret I don't know. As far as I know, we know everything about each other. Why won't he tell me his middle name. He doesn't have to tell me but it makes me feel bad that everybody else knows something about my best friend that I don't," said Ellen in Olly's head.

When Olly stood up straight after his reflection returned to normal, he and Ellen looked each other in the eyes.

"I'm sorry," they said at the same time.

Those two words were all it took to bring the friends back together. One word separated them and two brought them back. They both went on and on about how they now understand how the other feels. It finally ended when Olly whispered his middle name in Ellen's ear. She knew they would still be friends if he hadn't told her but she was glad he did. I would tell you all reading Olly's middle name but it wouldn't be right coming from me.

They said goodbye to Harrius as he hopped down the hill splashing water every which way as he hurried off to the library. By the way, he did make it there in time but had to pay a fine for the water damage to the book. He was used to that so he had his soggy money ready.

Olly and Ellen continued on their walk feeling as though they were even closer friends than before.

CHAPTER TEN

The Scales of Libra

Ellen would be starting school soon. She had already gone to get her new uniform and had almost all of the school supplies she would need. She picked out a red folder with a lion on it because it reminded her of Olly. Ellen liked school so she was excited about the new school year. She already knew her new teacher would be a nice woman named Mrs. Emerson so she didn't have to worry about that. Ellen only worried about one thing. She would have less time to visit Olly in the land of the Zodies.

The last time she was with Olly, Ellen explained that she would not be able to visit him as often because she would be busy with school. When Ellen received the playhouse that brought her to the land of the Zodies, it was summer and she had plenty of free time to travel back and forth between her world and Olly's. Olly did not like hearing that he wouldn't be able to see his best friend as often as he had been used to. He didn't like it one bit. Never had I heard a roar as loud as the one he roared after Ellen explained the situation. He said something had to be done about it but he needed time to figure out what that something was.

Before she left after telling Olly that her next visit would be her last before some time, they were both very sad saying goodbye to each other. They had always said goodbye but this one hurt their hearts to say it. They also knew the next goodbye would hurt even more because it would be a while before they could say hello again. There were tears in both eyes that they tried to hide from the other. Olly especially tried to hide his because for a Leo to cry would be unthinkable. He was no pussycat. He was a Leo. Even though he was sad, he was still a Leo. He waited for her playhouse to disappear before he shed any tears. Ellen's tears began as soon as she ran out of her playhouse and up to her room.

Ellen was sitting her in playhouse about to open the door. She had already opened her eyes after keeping them shut while dreaming of the land of the Zodies which caused her playhouse to transport her there. She opened the door slowly, expecting to see Olly standing there as he always was. This time he wasn't. Ellen thought this was very strange. Maybe Olly was playing hide and seek, she also thought. Ellen stepped outside and tripped over the Scales of Libra. The golden scales didn't seem phased by being tripped over but Ellen's right foot hurt a bit.

Ellen learned about the Scales of Libra on her previous trip to the land of the Zodies. The scales were the prize in the race of the Zodies. Every member of the zodiac participated in a race for procession of the scales. Olly had explained to Ellen that the Scales of Libra were the only thing that could bring all the members of the zodiac together.

It was quite a sight to see all the Zodies in one place, Ellen remembered. She wasn't the only spectator. Animals and magical creatures of all kind were lined up on either side of the makeshift course in the forest. Also in attendance were several gesundheits. Olly assured Ellen that on the day of the zodiac race, there is always peace so anyone was free to sneeze as much as they wanted. Running alongside the path was a river. In it she saw the Pisces sisters. The sisters were the second members of the Zodies Ellen had met after Olly when she first came to their world. Swimming practice laps next to the sisters was Betty the goat in her fish swimsuit. Betty was the Capricorn.

The rest of the Zodies were lined up next to each other on land. Starting from the opposite side Ellen was standing, the order was Rosa the ram, Toby the bull, Jim and Jenny Gemini, Mr. Fincher the crab, Olly, Virginia the Virgo, S.C. Orp the scorpion, Arnold the centaur and then Harrius the Aquarius.

Ellen had two honors that day. First, she was tasked

with holding the Scales of Libra during the race, although she was allowed to set it down as it was very heavy. The other honor being that she was selected to say the most important words at any race: Ready. Set. Go! As soon as Ellen shouted 'go', every Zodie took off running, crawling, galloping, hopping or swimming. I don't know what to call what Jim and Jenny Gemini took off doing considering they are a giant hand with an eyeball on top but their fingers got busy doing it.

Rosa the ram who was the Aries managed to talk endlessly about what a beautiful day it was for a race and how she was afraid they might be late because Betty couldn't find her fish swimsuit and Toby had smoke coming out of his nose because she was taking too long to find the perfect thing to wear to a race and how lovely it was that Ellen was there to watch them race and be able to hold the Scales of Libra and how lovely it was that Olly was taking the lead and what a good Leo he was and many more things as she raced along. The whole race was one long monologue about recent events in her life.

Toby the Taurus bull was doing his best to ignore his wife Rosa and concentrate on winning the race. For most this would be difficult to accomplish but Toby was a master at it. He was very focused on reaching the end of the path so he could turn around and make his way back and win. Some of the other Zodies were zigzagging across the path but Toby stayed in his own lane.

Jim and Jenny Gemini were running the race half-heartedly because their minds were on the fact they would have an exclusive interview with the winner after the race. They were always excited when it was time for the Zodie race because their interview with the winner was always a top seller of their newspaper. They had decided not to use their five W's and an H method like they used on Ellen once and instead use a traditional interviewing style. All the different questions they wanted to ask was all they could think about so it was no surprise that they were already in next to last place.

Mr. Fincher the Cancer crab was very unprepared because he was sure the race wasn't for another week. The morning of the race he woke up, had his breakfast and did some cleaning. He was surprised that he wasn't annoyed as usual by Olly who insisted on visiting the crabby crustacean whenever he was busy with something. Mr. Fincher then went to his jar of remembers to see if there was anything important for him to remember. When he finished reading the purple note with yellow circles, he crawled as fast as his eight legs could go. Surprisingly, he ended up being two hours early but stayed because he didn't want to risk going home and forgetting again. There he was, running in a race that he thought he had another week to prepare for. I don't think I'll ruin the story by telling you that Mr. Fincher doesn't win the race.

Olly roared at anybody who got close to getting ahead

of him as he was in the lead. He had won last year and was determined to win again.

Virginia the Virgo maiden was kindly letting the other racers pass by her as she thought just participating with her fellow Zodies was prize enough. She had already won as far as she was concerned. Virginia felt the experience was better than the outcome. When Toby almost knocked her down, she thanked him for reminding her to be careful.

When Olly realized that Virginia was allowing others to pass by, he thought this was very kind. He also thought this was very silly. He stopped and told her so, causing him to lose his lead but he felt it was his Leo duty to inform her of her foolishness. I don't think I'll surprise you by telling you that Virginia has never won a race of the Zodies.

S.C. Orp the Scorpio scorpion spent the whole race seeing how many questions he could ask himself before the race ended. As a champion questioner, he was unrivaled in his ability to ask an innumerable amount of questions. Leading up to the race, he practiced outside his home and had managed to ask himself 376 questions. By time he reached the halfway point on race day, Orp had asked himself 415 questions on a variety of subjects: What is the best recipe for meringue? Where do babies come from? What is the square root of pi times infinity plus two minus x? Why is Olly looking at me strangely? Orp asked himself the last question before he realized he was talking out loud and not to himself like he thought.

Arnold the Sagittarius centaur was galloping at a fast rate and was neck and neck with Olly for a time. Everyone else in the race wanted to win the Scales of Libra for the prestige and sense of accomplishment. Arnold wished so deeply that he would lose. Arnold had always been lucky and great things seemed to happen for him no matter how badly he didn't want them to. He was a frequent winner of the zodiac race but had lost last year to Olly. It was one of the happiest days of Arnold's life. He was hoping for a repeat loss.

Betty the Capricorn goat wearing a fish swimsuit was swimming along as fast as she could. She swam close to the bank because she promised her parents she would stay where they could see her. Each time she emerged from the water she would 'baa', then dive under again. Betty enjoyed swimming so much, that she several times forgot she was in a race and not just swimming for fun.

Harries the Aquarius hopped along in his jar, holding tight to the handles. He was creating patches of mud on the dirt path as water from his jar splashed out with every hop. At the beginning of the race it didn't cause a problem as he was in last place. By time he got within five feet of the turnaround point, everyone else rushed past him on their way back to the finish line.

Penelope and Isis Pisces always participated in the race. That isn't true. They always said they would but then they would show up and Isis would say she'd rather race in the opposite direction and when the race started, she'd take off down the opposite end of the stream. Penelope would always make it to the halfway point before realizing she had no use for the Scales of Libra and swim home from there.

As the racers made their way towards the finish line, they all began to slip and slide into each other as they fell victim to the sloppy mud patches caused by Harrius's overflow. Betty stopped swimming when she heard the commotion coming from land. Olly was usually good at steering clear of such obstacles but when a bull slams into you from behind, it's difficult to keep your mind on a race. Ellen looked on in amazement at the pile of Zodies covered in mud. She then looked over and saw Harrius hopping towards the pile of his fellow Zodies. He stopped just in front of them, held tight to his handles, and hopped a hop so high that he soared over the group and landed before the finish line. Harrius took two more hops forward and won the race.

Ellen couldn't help but smile as she remembered the race standing outside her playhouse looking down at the Scales of Libra she had just tripped over. She decided to go searching for Olly who wasn't there to greet her as he usually was. The Scales of Libra were heavy, Ellen remembered so she alternated carrying it and pulling it behind her as she started off. She tried to think of where Olly could be or what he was doing that kept him from being at her door when she arrived. She had been walking for a few minutes when she noticed the scales getting lighter and so was she. Ellen looked down because her feet no longer felt the ground beneath them. The ground was still there but she was high above it as the Scales were taking flight and taking her along, too.

The Scales flew over the land of the Zodies with Ellen hanging on tightly. Eventually, it hovered over a circle shaped building that looked made of gold. The Scales of Libra set Ellen then itself down gently in front of two large doors. Ellen knocked and immediately the doors opened to one large round room with a large round table. Around the table was every member of the zodiac. In front of the table was Olly. As soon as she walked in, they all shouted.

"SURPRISE!!" exclaimed all the Zodies.

Olly told Ellen that since she wouldn't be visiting the Land of the Zodies as often, everyone wanted to do something nice for her and Olly decided a surprise party was the best idea and everyone agreed because he was the Leo and that was that. There was cake and ice cream and other delicious treats. Ellen remembered Olly telling her before the race that the Scales of Libra was the only thing that brought all the Zodies together yet here they all were. Every one of them was there for her. Even the Pisces sisters were there in their bubbles.

Ellen would remember this day for this rest of her life. She knew it wasn't a goodbye forever party. It was just a until next time party. Ellen of course went on to have many more adventures in the Land of the Zodies. They were only less frequent. In a way, it made the time she did spend there with Olly even more special because she had gone longer without visiting.

Back in her world, as Ellen would be doing her homework, she would look out the back window and stare at her playhouse. The sight of it in the backyard always gave her inspiration to work hard so that her parents would be okay with her going out and having a quick play inside. Of course they never knew a quick play in our world was an adventure in the Land of the Zodies.

Until next time.

ABOUT THE AUTHOR

Emmanuel King is the chief executive officer of a security software company. He grew up as an only child with a powerful imagination that could transport him far away. He lives in Washington, D.C.

Printed in the United States
By Bookmasters